# The
# Hidden Treasures

Nancy ran her hand over the wall. When she touched one of the bricks, it moved a tiny bit. Nancy slid it out.

"I'll bet there's something in there," George said.

Nancy shone a flashlight in the hole. "There is," she said. She reached in and pulled out the object.

"It's a book," George said. "What's the title?"

Nancy held out the book for Bess and George to see. On the front were gold letters that said, "My Diary."

"What are we waiting for?" Bess said. Her blue eyes sparkled with excitement. "Let's read it!"

## The Nancy Drew Notebooks

Available from MINSTREL Books

# THE
# NANCY DREW
# NOTEBOOKS®

#24

*The Hidden Treasures*

CAROLYN KEENE
ILLUSTRATED BY ANTHONY ACCARDO

A MINSTREL® BOOK

Published by POCKET BOOKS
New York   London   Toronto   Sydney   Tokyo   Singapore

This book is a work of fiction. Names, characters, places and incidents are products of the author's imagination or are used fictitiously. Any resemblance to actual events or locales or persons living or dead is entirely coincidental.

A MINSTREL PAPERBACK *Original*

 A Minstrel Book published by
POCKET BOOKS, a division of Simon & Schuster Inc.
1230 Avenue of the Americas, New York, NY 10020

Copyright © 1998 by Simon & Schuster Inc.
Produced by Mega-Books, Inc.

ISBN: 0-671-00819-6

First Minstrel Books printing May 1998

10  9  8  7  6  5  4  3

NANCY DREW, THE NANCY DREW NOTEBOOKS, A MINSTREL BOOK and colophon are registered trademarks of Simon & Schuster Inc.

Cover art by Joanie Schwarz

Printed in the U.S.A.

# 1

## A
## Hidden Surprise

You have to help me!" Nancy Drew cried. "I just can't decide who to do my report on."

Nancy was walking home from school with Bess Marvin and George Fayne. They were going to Nancy's house after school. Bess and George were cousins. They were Nancy's best friends.

"You'd better think quickly," Bess said. "We have to tell Mrs. Reynolds our topics tomorrow."

The girls were in the same third-grade class at Carl Sandburg Elementary School in River Heights. Their teacher, Mrs. Reynolds, had given them a social studies assignment. Each student had to do an oral report on someone from their state of Illinois.

Nancy thought it would be fun to do a report on someone from her own state. But she couldn't decide whom to pick.

"Why don't you choose someone famous, like I did?" Bess said. "I'm doing my report on Abraham Lincoln. He was the sixteenth president of the United States. And he was from Illinois."

"I picked Carl Sandburg," George said. "He's pretty famous here at Carl Sandburg Elementary School."

"Very funny!" Nancy laughed at George's joke.

"How about Mary Todd?" Bess asked. "She was Abraham Lincoln's wife."

"That's a good idea," Nancy said. "But I'd like to do my report on someone different. Someone nobody knows."

Bess laughed. "How are you going to find someone nobody knows?"

"I mean someone who wasn't famous," Nancy answered. "Maybe Hannah can think of someone," she said as they walked up to her house.

Hannah Gruen was the Drews' housekeeper.

"Hello, girls," Hannah called. "The workers are almost finished for today."

Just then two men in overalls carried a kitchen cabinet out the back door.

"Nancy!" Bess said. "You're not moving, are you?"

"No, we're not moving," Nancy answered with a laugh. "I forgot to tell you we're getting a new kitchen floor and new cabinets, though. We're also getting the kitchen painted. It's going to be a mess for a while."

Nancy, Bess, and George walked into the kitchen. Nancy looked at the wall where the old cabinets had been. Instead of a white plaster wall, it was now brick.

"Wow!" Nancy exclaimed. "Did the

3

workers put in that brick wall, Hannah?"

"No," Hannah said. "The brick wall was there first. When the workers took down the cabinets, they took off the old plaster, too," she explained. "Underneath, we discovered the brick wall."

Nancy ran her hand over the wall. She could feel that one of the bricks was sticking out. When she touched it, it moved a tiny bit.

"Look at this," she called to Bess and George. Nancy pulled on the brick. The brick slid out.

"I'll bet there's something in there," George said.

Nancy took a flashlight from a drawer and shone it in the hole. "There *is* something in there," she said. "It's red."

"Don't put your hand in there!" Bess cried. "You'll get all dirty."

Nancy smiled at her friend. "Don't worry, Bess. I'll wash my hands later." She reached in again and felt around. "I've got it," she said. She pulled out the red object and held it up.

4

"It's a book," George said. "What's the title?"

Nancy held out the book for Bess and George to see. On the front were gold letters that said, "My Diary."

"It looks old," George said.

The diary was made of red leather and had a rusty latch on it. Nancy pushed on the latch until it sprang open. Then she turned to the first page.

"Listen to this," Nancy said. She read from the first page: " 'This diary belongs to Amelia Barton, 1943.' "

"That's more than fifty years ago!" George said.

"Amelia Barton left this diary here fifty years ago?" Bess said.

"I guess so," Nancy said. "That also means that Amelia Barton lived in this house."

# 2

# Amelia's Mystery

**B**ut why did Amelia stick her diary in the wall—where it would get covered up forever?'' George asked.

"Maybe she explains in the diary," Nancy said.

"What are we waiting for?" Bess said. Her blue eyes sparkled with excitement. "Let's read it!"

The girls ran to the living room and plopped down on the couch. Nancy began to read.

"BEWARE! Anyone who reads my diary will have to live in the attic

FOREVER and be haunted by ghosts.
(Especially you, Edward.)

"Do you think it's okay to read the diary?" Bess asked.

"Sure," Nancy said. "We don't believe in ghosts, do we?"

"I don't think so," Bess said slowly.

"I wonder who Edward is," George said.

"Let's read some more," Nancy said. She turned to the first entry and began to read.

"January 1, 1943.
Dear Diary: Happy New Year! And happy new diary—my very first one. I got it for Christmas. It's red, my very favorite color. Mother told me to write down what was important to me. But I'm only eight years old. Nothing important ever happens to me."

"Hey! She's eight, the same age as we are," George said.

"Lots of important stuff happens to us," Bess said.

"Yes, like finding an old diary," Nancy said. She began reading again.

"Mother said just to write anything I want. She said a diary is private. That means secret. But Edward, the brat, doesn't know what private means. (I wonder if all little brothers are brats.) I know he would read my diary if he could. So I found a good place to hide it—behind a loose brick in the kitchen wall."

"Now we know who Edward is," George said. "Amelia's brother."

"And we know why she hid the diary behind a loose brick in the kitchen," Nancy said. "She wanted to hide it from Edward."

"Let me read now," Bess said. Nancy handed her the book, and Bess found her place.

"I will show my diary to Elizabeth and Ruth because they are my two best

9

friends. They are sisters. They live around the corner and down a few streets. Their father is in the army. People who are in the army move around a lot. Elizabeth and Ruth moved here two years ago. I hope they don't move now that there's a war going on."

"What war is she talking about?" Bess asked.

"Let's ask Hannah," Nancy said.

The girls ran to the kitchen to show Hannah the entry in the diary.

"Amelia is talking about World War Two," Hannah told them. "That's when the United States and several other countries fought against Germany and Japan and Italy."

"I have a great idea, Nancy," Bess said. "You can do your report on Amelia."

"You're right, Bess!" Nancy clapped her hands with excitement. "I wanted to do my report on someone different. Amelia is *really* different."

"I wonder if we can figure out where Elizabeth and Ruth lived," George said.

"Maybe we can," Nancy said. "There might be more clues in the diary."

"Come on," Bess said. "Let's read the rest of it." She pulled the other two upstairs to Nancy's room.

Bess and Nancy sat on Nancy's bed. George sat on Nancy's rug next to the bed.

"My turn to read," George said.

"January 5.
Dear Diary: Elizabeth and Ruth came over today. We played dress-up in the attic, and I showed them my new diary. The attic is a perfect place to play because Edward never goes up there. He thinks there are ghosts in the attic. He's afraid of the basement, too, but I don't know why."

"I have an idea," Nancy said. "Let's go up to the attic and read the diary. It will be spookier up there."

"I'm not sure," Bess said.

"Cool!" George said.

On their way to the attic, Nancy stubbed her toe on something. "Ow!" she said. A nail was sticking up from the top stair. "Watch out for that nail," she told the others. She tapped the nail down with the heel of her shoe so that it would stay in place.

Nancy opened the attic door. The girls dusted off a large box and sat down. Then they took turns reading the diary. They read all about what it was like to grow up in River Heights in 1943. Amelia and her friends had gone to the same school that Nancy, Bess, and George did.

Nancy, Bess, and George read all the way to the June entries. They were having so much fun that they lost track of time.

"Uh-oh," Bess said. "I wonder what time it is."

"My stomach is growling," George said. "I'll bet it's close to dinnertime."

"Let me read just one more entry to you," Nancy said. "You have to hear this."

"June 1.
Dear Diary: Bad news. Next month Elizabeth and Ruth are moving away from River Heights. The army is making their father go to another town because of the war. We promised to write each other every week. But I don't know if we will ever see each other again."

"Oh, no," Bess said. "This is so sad."
"Wait, there's more," Nancy said.

"We decided to do something special before Elizabeth and Ruth leave. We are each going to hide something that reminds us of our friendship. They will be our hidden treasures. Ruth's treasure is from me. I made it with a heart that fell off one of Mother's old pins. Elizabeth's treasure belonged to Aunt Tillie, who was also one of her best friends. (It looks just like Aunt Tillie, too!) My treasure is a gift Grandma gave me when I was little. Now we have to decide where to hide our treasures."

"Skip ahead," George said eagerly. "Let's see where they hid them."

Nancy turned several pages. She began to read.

"July 6.
Dear Diary: Elizabeth and Ruth are moving two days from today, so we hid our treasures yesterday. We decided a loose brick is the best hiding place. (That's where I hide my diary from Edward.) No one ever thinks of looking behind a brick. So Ruth put hers under the new statue of Carl Sandburg in the library park. Elizabeth hid hers under her gazebo. Mine is in the house, where Edward the brat is afraid to go!"

Nancy looked through the next few pages. "That's strange," she said. "Amelia stopped writing in her diary. I wonder why."

"Read the last entry," George said. "Maybe that will give us a clue."

"August 6.
Dear Diary: Edward and I are going to Grandma's house until school starts.

Daddy is making the kitchen bigger, and Mother says it will be too messy around here. I am leaving my diary at home. There isn't any place to hide it at Grandma's, and I know Edward will read it. I'll write all about my trip when I get back."

"Now I know why the diary was never finished," Nancy said. "Amelia hid her diary behind a loose brick in the kitchen wall, right?"

"Right," Bess said, nodding her head.

"Well, Amelia put it there before she went to her grandmother's," Nancy went on. "Then her parents fixed up the kitchen."

"That's right," George said. "After that, Amelia couldn't get to her diary anymore."

The girls sat in silence for a moment. "I'm sorry the diary ended early," Nancy said. "I like Amelia. I feel as if I know her."

Bess nodded. "Me, too. I also like Elizabeth and Ruth. I'm sad they had to move."

"You know," Nancy said slowly, "I was wondering if the treasures are still in their hiding places."

"Do you think so?" George asked with a gasp. "They were hidden fifty years ago."

"And we don't even know what the treasures are," Bess said.

"But there are clues in the diary," Nancy replied. "And we haven't read the whole thing yet."

She jumped up from the box. "I think it would be a great idea if we tried to find the treasures."

"Okay," Bess said.

"Okay for me, too," George said. "When do we start?"

"Well, tomorrow's Friday," Nancy said. "We could start right after school!"

# 3

# The Treasure Hunt Begins

That evening Nancy's father, Carson Drew, brought pizza home for dinner. "We might have to order in or eat out until the kitchen is finished," he told Nancy and Hannah.

"Sounds good to me," Nancy said as she bit into a steaming-hot slice of pizza.

"I don't mind, either," Hannah said. "I won't miss cooking for a while."

Hannah set the table in the dining room. She used paper plates and plastic forks, knives, and spoons.

"This is like having an indoor picnic," Nancy said.

"Without the ants," Hannah added.

Over dinner Nancy told her father about finding the diary behind a brick in the kitchen wall.

"The diary belonged to a girl named Amelia Barton," Nancy told him eagerly. "And guess what? She was my age when she wrote it."

"She began the diary in 1943," Hannah added.

"I wonder what happened to Amelia," Nancy said.

"I'll bet we can find out," Mr. Drew said.

"How?" Nancy asked.

"There are a few different ways. You could ask some of our neighbors," Mr. Drew said. "Mrs. Ratazchek grew up in this neighborhood. She might remember Amelia and where she moved. We can also look for her on the computer."

"The computer?" Nancy said. "Where would we begin?"

"There are Web sites that combine all the phone books in the country. I'll show you how to find them over the weekend," Mr. Drew said.

"Okay," Nancy said happily. "Gee, if we could find Amelia . . ." Suddenly she put down her cup of soda and frowned.

"What's wrong?" Mr. Drew asked. "Don't you want to find Amelia?"

Nancy swallowed and took a deep breath. "Yes," she said slowly. "But . . . would she be angry at me for reading her diary?"

Mr. Drew smiled. "I doubt it, Pudding Pie."

"Pudding Pie" was Mr. Drew's special name for Nancy.

"Amelia is a grown woman now," Mr. Drew continued. "She wrote her diary a long time ago."

"If you think it's okay," Nancy said, "I feel better now." She took a last bite of her pizza.

After dinner Nancy ran upstairs and put on her nightgown. It was white with red and pink roses on it. Then she curled up in bed with the diary.

She also took out her special blue notebook. That's where she always

wrote down clues when she was trying to solve a mystery.

Nancy opened her notebook to a fresh page. On the top she wrote, "The Hidden Treasures." Under that she made two columns. In one column she listed Amelia's, Elizabeth's, and Ruth's names. Beside each girl's name she wrote a description of her treasure. Then she turned to the diary again.

As she read, Nancy looked for all the places in the diary that mentioned the treasures. When she found a clue, she wrote it down in her notebook.

Nancy was still reading the diary when her father came upstairs to tell her it was time for bed.

"Good night, Daddy," Nancy said when he kissed her on top of her head. "I'll finish tomorrow," she said as her father turned out the light.

The next day Nancy couldn't wait to tell Mrs. Reynolds about Amelia's diary.

"Amelia sounds like a wonderful subject," Mrs. Reynolds said. "Just make sure there's enough material in the diary for your report," she said. "You may need to go to the library to find out more about World War Two, for example."

"What's this about a diary?" a voice said behind Nancy. Nancy turned around quickly. Brenda Carlton was standing there.

"I heard you talking to Mrs. Reynolds," Brenda said. "Let me see the diary so I can write a story about it in my newspaper."

Brenda's father owned a newspaper. He helped Brenda put out her own newspaper, called the *Carlton News*. Brenda wrote the newspaper on the computer.

Nancy frowned. "You can do an article, Brenda," she said. "But I can't let you see the diary. You'll have to wait for my report."

Brenda tossed her long, dark hair back over her shoulder. "I'll find out about the diary somehow," she said. "Just look for it in your favorite local newspaper, the *Carlton News*."

"I can't wait, Brenda," Nancy said as she took her seat.

Right after school the three friends headed straight for the library. Nancy told Bess and George about writing down the clues she found in the diary.

"I think we should look for Ruth's treasure first," Nancy said. "It will be the easiest to find because we have all the clues."

"Since we're going to the library, we can look up some stuff for our reports there," George said.

"Tell us again," Bess said. "Where was Ruth's treasure hidden?"

"Under the statue of Carl Sandburg," Nancy answered.

Just as they walked into the library, Nancy had the feeling someone was behind them. She turned around and saw Brenda coming up the sidewalk.

Nancy pulled George and Bess over to the checkout desk. "Brenda's following us," she whispered. "Quick, let's hide."

She hurried toward a row of bookshelves. Bess and George were right behind her.

"Wait!" Nancy said. She stopped so suddenly that Bess and George almost knocked her down.

"Ow!" Bess cried. "Why did you stop?"

"Look!" Nancy pointed to a door with a sign: The Carl Sandburg Room. "Let's hide in here," she said.

Nancy opened the door. The girls slipped inside and closed the door.

"I hope she didn't see us," Bess said. She backed away from the door.

"Oops!" She bumped into a table in the middle of the room. "Sorry!" she said. Then she turned around. When she saw the table, she began to giggle. Nancy and George began to laugh, too.

Bess pointed to a small statue on the table. "That's Carl Sandburg," she said.

Nancy's eyes lit up. The girls walked around the table, looking at the statue closely.

"I don't see where a treasure would be." Bess shrugged.

"Didn't the diary say it was under

the statue?" George asked. "Well, maybe the treasure is under the table."

"Let's look," Nancy said. The girls got down on their hands and knees and crawled under the table. Bess craned her neck up and peered underneath the table. Suddenly the door opened.

"What are you girls doing?" a loud voice demanded. "You're not supposed to be in here without special permission."

# 4

# The
# Statue's Secret

Bess got up quickly and bumped her head on the table. "Ow!" she cried. She rubbed her head.

Nancy peeked out from under the desk. She recognized Brenda Carlton's legs in the doorway. Next to Brenda was another pair of legs. Nancy looked up. Her heart sank. The other legs belonged to Mrs. Green, the librarian.

"What are you girls doing under the table?" Mrs. Green asked.

"Uh . . ." Bess began.

"Well . . . we . . ." George said.

"I dropped my pencil," Nancy said. "I thought it rolled under the table."

No one wanted to tell Mrs. Green that they were hiding from Brenda.

Mrs. Green looked at them and raised one eyebrow. "I see," she said. "Did you forget that you're supposed to ask permission to come in here?"

"Yes, we forgot," Nancy said. "We're sorry."

Mrs. Green guided them out of the room. "That's okay. Just don't forget next time."

"I feel terrible," Bess said to Nancy and George. "We didn't tell the truth."

"I know," Nancy said. "We couldn't really explain anything. If we did, Brenda would know what we were looking for."

"You know Brenda told on us," George said angrily. She looked over her shoulder. "And she's still following us."

"I know how we can lose Brenda," Nancy said. "I'm going to pretend I lost the diary. You pretend with me." She led Bess and George into an aisle between two bookcases.

Peeking through a shelf, they could see Brenda in the next aisle. Her hand was cupped over her ear so she could hear what they said.

"She's so nosy!" Bess whispered loudly.

Then Nancy took a deep breath. "I don't know what to do," she said. "I lost the old diary yesterday."

"Where did you go?" George asked.

"Well, after school I went to the *Sugar 'n' Spice* for ice cream," Nancy said. She said "Sugar 'n' Spice" louder and slower than the rest of her words.

"Then I went to the *town park* to eat my ice cream. Oh, yes, then I went to the *Double Dip* for another ice cream."

"Didn't you go to the *post office* to mail a letter, too?" Bess said,

"Oh, yes, I forgot," Nancy said. "And I went to the *drug store,* too. I could have left the diary at any of those places."

"We'll help you look for it," George said.

In a moment the girls saw Brenda hurrying out the front door of the library.

"There she goes." Bess giggled. Nancy and George started giggling, too. Soon they were bursting with laughter.

"Shh!" A man reading a newspaper put a finger to his lips. The girls put their hands over their mouths to hold in their laughter.

Next the girls did some research for their oral reports. Nancy looked up the dates for World War II in the *World Almanac*. George found a biography of Carl Sandburg, and Bess found some photographs of Abraham Lincoln that she was able to photocopy.

At the checkout desk, Nancy asked if there was another statue of Carl Sandburg in the library.

"No," Mrs. Green told them, "but there's one in the town park."

"Did the diary say anything about the town park?" Bess asked Nancy.

"I don't think so," Nancy said, looking in her blue notebook.

Her face broke into a smile. "Oh! The

31

statue isn't in the library. It's in the library *park*. But how can that be?"

"Wait a second, girls," Mrs. Green said. "I think I can help you." She walked toward the Carl Sandburg Room, then stopped at the door.

"You can come in, girls," she said to Nancy, Bess, and George. "You have permission."

Mrs. Green took a large book off a shelf. "This book tells the history of River Heights," she said. She flipped through the pages. "Here's what I was looking for." She read from the book for a moment.

"There used to be a statue of Carl Sandburg in the little park outside the library. Now the statue is here in this room. If you look outside, you'll find the original pedestal that the statue stood on."

"Thank you, Mrs. Green," Nancy said.

Nancy, Bess, and George walked quickly to the back door of the library and outside to the park.

There the girls found a neat pile of bricks that were cemented together.

They formed a base about three feet high. Nancy bent over and looked at a gold-colored plate attached to one side of the base.

"I found it," Nancy called. "Listen to what this says. 'Carl Sandburg—Illinois Poet.'"

"What should we do?" Bess asked.

George stood up straight. "If the diary says the treasure was under the statue, then it could be here."

"That's right," Nancy said. "And remember Amelia wrote that the best place to hide something was behind a loose brick."

The girls kneeled down and looked at all the bricks very carefully. Sure enough, one of the bottom bricks was loose. Nancy pulled it out.

"Who's going to stick her hand in this time?" Nancy asked.

"Not me," Bess said.

"I'll do it," George said. "I'd love to find the first treasure."

George took a deep breath and put her hand inside the hole. "I feel something!" she cried.

She pulled her hand out and slowly opened her palm. The girls all gasped. She was holding a ring made out of tin with a red glass heart on it.

"It's Ruth's hidden treasure," Nancy said softly. "There's the heart Amelia used from her mom's pin."

"This is amazing!" Bess said. "It's been here for fifty years!"

George slipped the ring on her finger. "It fits! Do you think it's okay if I wear it?"

"Of course," Nancy said. "You found it."

"That means if we find all the treasures, we can each have one," George said. "We're lucky there are three treasures."

"Whose treasure do you think we should look for next, Nancy?" Bess asked.

"I think we should look for Elizabeth's treasure," Nancy answered. "Come over tomorrow, and we'll figure out what to do."

"Yeah!" Bess cheered.

By then it was nearly dinnertime, and the girls headed for their homes.

As she was turning down her block, Nancy saw Mrs. Ratazchek coming toward her. Her neighbor was taking a walk with another woman.

"Hello, Nancy," Mrs. Ratazchek said. "Do you remember my mother?"

"Yes, I do," Nancy answered.

"Hello, dear," Mrs. Ratazchek's mother said.

"Mrs. Ratazchek," Nancy began, "do you remember a girl named Amelia Barton? She lived in my house before my family did."

"The name *Barton* is familiar," Mrs. Ratazchek said. "But I don't remember Amelia."

"I do," Mrs. Ratazchek's mother said. "She and her brother, Edward, were about my age."

"You actually knew them?" Nancy said. "Do you know what happened to them?"

"Let's see." Mrs. Ratazchek's mother thought for a moment. "They both grew up and moved away. Edward got married and moved to Chicago. Amelia got married and moved, too. But I don't know where. I'm sorry."

"That's okay," Nancy said. "That's a big help. Thanks."

That evening Mr. Drew took Nancy and Hannah out to dinner. Nancy ordered an open-face turkey sandwich. "This is just like Thanksgiving," she said. She took a forkful of cranberry sauce.

Over dinner Nancy told her father and Hannah about what Mrs. Rataz-chek's mother had said. "If Amelia Barton got married, then wouldn't she have a different last name now?" she asked. "Before Mrs. Reynolds got married, her name was Ms. Spencer."

"Very good thinking," Mr. Drew said. "You are really using your detective skills, Nancy. Amelia Barton probably does have a different name now. But even if Edward got married, he would still have the same last name. So maybe the way to find Amelia is to find Edward first."

"We're a good detective team," Nancy said.

"We certainly are," Mr. Drew answered.

After they returned home Nancy rushed upstairs and stretched out on her bed. She was eager to finish reading the diary. In one entry she came across a clue that was so amazing it made her drop the diary.

She wrote the new clue in her blue notebook exactly as she had read it in the diary: "Aunt Tillie is buried in Elizabeth and Ruth's backyard."

I can't wait to tell George and Bess about *this!* Nancy thought.

# 5

## A
## Surprising Clue

**N**ancy woke up Saturday morning thinking about the surprising clue she had read the night before. But a delicious smell made her think about breakfast instead.

She headed for the kitchen, where she and her father usually had breakfast. She was looking forward to the pancakes her father liked to make on Saturdays. Then Nancy remembered there was no kitchen.

She sighed. That meant no pancakes, either. We're probably having cold cereal again, Nancy thought. She decided she would be happy when the kitchen was back to normal.

Mr. Drew was sitting at the dining room table. In front of him was a plate heaped with warm cinnamon buns. Nancy's face broke into a huge smile.

"I used the toaster oven to heat these up," Mr. Drew said. "By the way, I found something on our doorstep this morning."

Nancy's smile disappeared when her father handed her a copy of the *Carlton News,* Brenda's newspaper.

The headline on the front page read, "Local Girls Caught Sneaking into Carl Sandburg Room." Brenda had written a story about Mrs. Green finding Nancy, Bess, and George under the table with the statue of Carl Sandburg on it.

Nancy began to laugh. "We were just trying to find a treasure we read about in Amelia's diary," she told her father. "And we did."

She put a cinnamon bun on her plate while Mr. Drew poured her some orange juice. "We couldn't tell Mrs. Green what we were doing because nosy Brenda was there."

Mr. Drew listened to Nancy's story with a smile on his face. "When you finish breakfast," he said, "we'll pull up the Chicago directory on my computer. Maybe we can find Edward's address."

Nancy drank her orange juice and jumped up eagerly. "Okay, I'm finished!"

While Nancy and Mr. Drew were looking through the Chicago listings, Mrs. Marvin dropped off Bess and George.

"Guess what? Dad and I just found Edward's address and phone number on the computer," Nancy said. She pointed to the screen. "There are twenty-seven Bartons in Chicago, but only one whose first name is Edward."

"Did you find Amelia's name?" George asked.

"No, not yet," Nancy said. "But if she got married, she might have a different last name."

Bess and George followed Nancy

through the dining room on their way upstairs. Bess saw the *Carlton News* on the dining room table. "We got copies of that awful paper today, too," she said angrily. "Brenda sure makes up a good story."

George shook her head. "Oh, well. We didn't tell her the truth. She had to write *something*."

"Where should we start looking for Elizabeth's treasure, Nancy?" Bess said.

"Oh, I almost forgot." Nancy's eyes lit up. "You won't believe what I read in the diary last night!"

"Ooh, what?" Bess said.

"Amelia wrote that Aunt Tillie died and was buried in Elizabeth and Ruth's backyard," Nancy said.

"No way!" George exclaimed. "Their aunt is buried in their backyard?"

Nancy opened her notebook and read from it. " 'We buried Aunt Tillie in her favorite spot, between the cherry tree and the gazebo.' "

"I wonder if she's still there," Bess said, her eyes wide.

"Hmm. A gazebo," George said. "There

are two gazebos in our neighborhood. One is in Mr. Randolph's backyard, and the other is in Jason Hutchings's."

Bess started giggling. "I wonder how Jason would feel about having someone's Aunt Tillie buried in his backyard."

"Which yard should we go to first?" Bess said.

"Well," Nancy began, "I've been thinking. Mr. Randolph doesn't have a tree in his backyard. But Jason does."

"I just thought of something, too," George said. "If we find the treasure at Jason's, then it means that Elizabeth and Ruth used to live in Jason's house."

"I just hope Brenda doesn't follow us there, too," Nancy said. "Next she'll write a story about us sneaking into Jason's yard!"

"We may have to sneak in," George said. "It's Saturday, remember? So Jason might be home."

The girls sat on Nancy's bed. How could they get into Jason's yard to look for the treasure?

Nancy jumped up. "I know how we can get into Jason's yard. We'll take Chip."

Chocolate Chip was Nancy's chocolate-colored Labrador retriever.

"Will Chip sniff out the treasure?" Bess asked.

"Sort of," Nancy said. "I'll take some dog treats. Then, when we get to Jason's, I'll throw one in his backyard."

"Great idea!" George said. "Then Chip will run into the yard to get it."

"Yes," Nancy said. "And then we'll have to go get Chip. I'll catch Chip, and you both can look around the yard."

"That could work," George said.

"I think so, too," Bess said.

Nancy knocked on the door to her father's study and told him that they were taking Chip for a walk. Then she hooked Chip's leash onto the dog's red collar, and the girls headed for Jason's house.

As they walked past Jason's back fence, Nancy tossed a treat into the backyard. The girls stopped so Chip could run after the treat. But the puppy sat down and looked up at Nancy, wagging her tail.

Nancy tugged gently on her dog's leash. "Get up, Chip!" she whispered. "Come on, girl!"

"Give her a treat to eat," George whispered. "Then throw another one into the yard."

"Hurry!" Bess whispered. "Someone will see us standing here."

Nancy bent down and let Chip sniff another treat. After Chip lapped it up she threw another one into Jason's yard. Chip put her front paws on the fence.

"Oh, no! She won't jump," Nancy said. "We'll have to open the gate."

They tiptoed to the back gate and opened it quietly. Nancy threw another dog treat into the yard, and Chip ran to get it.

"Finally!" Nancy sighed.

The girls followed Chip in. Nancy caught Chip by her collar and started petting her. Quickly Bess and George ran to the gazebo. They searched the grass around the gazebo as quickly as they could.

Suddenly Bess let out a loud scream. "I just found Aunt Tillie's gravestone!"

# 6

# In Jason's
# Backyard

**B**ess pointed to a brick in the gaze-bo's foundation. The initials *A.T.* were carved on it. "*A.T.* must stand for Aunt Tillie," she cried. "Aunt Tillie's buried here!"

Just then the back door to Jason's house flew open, and Jason came running out.

"Hey!" he said when he saw the girls. "What are you doing in my yard?"

"Well, you cut through everybody's yard on your way to school every day," Bess said.

"Do not," Jason said.

"Do so," Nancy said.

Jason looked down at George. George was still on her hands and knees. "What are you looking for?" he asked suspiciously.

George jumped up. "Nothing," she said quickly.

"Chip ran into your backyard, and we came to get her," Nancy said.

"Oh, yeah?" Jason said. "Then why did Bess scream?"

"I . . . I thought I saw . . ." Bess began.

Just then Mrs. Hutchings stuck her head out the back door. "Jason, we have to leave for the dentist now," she called out.

"Hello, Mrs. Hutchings," Nancy called.

"Oh, hello, Nancy," Mrs. Hutchings said, smiling. "What are you girls up to?"

"Um, we're just trying to catch my dog," Nancy said. She tried not to sound nervous. "Chip ran into your yard."

"Okay, dear," Mrs. Hutchings said.

Then she headed for her car, which was parked in the driveway.

"I'm sorry we have to go," she said. "Jason has a dentist appointment."

"Oh, that's okay," Nancy said. She pulled on Chip's leash. "We were going anyway."

"As if we would come here to visit Jason," Bess said under her breath.

The girls followed Jason out the back gate. When he got into the car, he rolled down his window and leaned out. "I still want to know why you were sneaking around in my yard," he said.

The girls watched Mrs. Hutchings back out and drive around the corner. Then Nancy said, "We're going back. We have to check out the bricks under the gazebo. That's where Elizabeth's treasure is."

Bess shuddered. "Why do we have to?"

"Because the diary said Elizabeth's treasure was *under* the gazebo," Nancy said. "We have to look for a loose brick."

The girls went back into the yard.

"Look!" Nancy said. "The brick with *A.T.* on it is sticking out a little. See if you can get it out, Bess."

Bess gasped. "But what about Aunt Tillie?"

"This isn't a gravestone, silly," Nancy said. "Aunt Tillie was buried in the yard, remember, not under the gazebo."

"I took out the last brick, Bess," George said. "Don't you want to find one of the treasures?"

Bess squinched up her nose and pushed the brick with one finger. It moved a little. "It *is* loose," Bess whispered excitedly.

Bess pushed the brick back and forth with her fingertips. After a moment it was out. "I did it!" she said proudly.

"Good work," Nancy said. "Now see if anything's in the hole."

Bess swallowed. "I just know there's a worm in there." Then she closed her eyes and slowly slid her hand inside the opening.

"I feel something," she said. She pulled her hand out and opened her eyes. "Look! It's a necklace!" she shouted happily.

But before Nancy and George could look at the treasure, they heard the Hutchingses' car drive up. Nancy grabbed Chip. Then she and George and Bess all ducked down behind the gazebo.

"Oh, no! We forgot!" George whispered, nodding toward the yard. Nancy looked over. She saw the brick with *A.T.* on it lying in the grass. "What if Jason sees it?"

Jason got out of the car and came through the gate. "Wait! I see something, Mom," he yelled, heading toward the gazebo. The girls crouched down, holding their breath.

To Nancy's horror, Chip began growling softly. Quickly Nancy shoved her hand into her pocket and took out a dog treat. She held it out for Chip to sniff. The puppy thumped her tail happily.

Jason ran up the gazebo steps. "Here they are, Mom!" he called out.

He's seen us, Nancy thought. What am I going to tell his mother?

Then Jason ran back down the stairs waving a pair of gloves. The girls heard the door slam shut and the car back out of the driveway.

As soon as the car was gone, George jumped up and shoved the *A.T.* brick back into place. "Let's go before they come back *again*."

The girls ran through the gate and down the front sidewalk. They didn't stop until they were in front of Nancy's house.

The girls flopped down on the front lawn. "Whew!" Bess panted. "That was *too* close." She pulled the necklace out of her pocket. Hanging from it was a silver charm.

"It's a dog," George said.

Nancy frowned. "But Amelia wrote that the charm looked just like Aunt Tillie. That wasn't a very nice thing to say."

Bess turned the charm over. "There's something written on the back. It says,

'My name is Aunt Tillie. If you find me lost, take me home to . . . ' "

Bess laughed. "Hey! It's Jason's address." Then her mouth dropped open. "This is a dog tag!" she cried. "Aunt Tillie was a dog!"

# 7

# The Secret
# under the Stair

You mean Aunt Tillie was Elizabeth's dog?" George said. "Not her aunt?"

Bess nodded her head. She couldn't say anything because she was laughing so hard. Nancy burst out laughing, too. George couldn't hold herself back.

After a minute Bess put the necklace around her neck. She looked down at it.

"I have to go home now," George said. "It's my mom's turn to pick us up, and she and my dad are going out tonight."

"Let's look for Amelia's treasure to-morrow," Bess said. "We know it's at your house, Nancy."

"Okay," Nancy agreed. "And we can work on our oral reports, too."

Bess and George arrived at Nancy's early Sunday afternoon. "Which comes first?" Nancy asked. "Report or treasure?"

"Treasure!" Bess and George both said.

"Where do we start?" Bess asked.

"Amelia's treasure is probably behind a brick, too," Nancy said. "That's where she hid her diary. So let's look at the kitchen wall first."

The girls felt all the bricks they could reach, but none of them was loose.

Nancy checked her blue notebook for clues. "It has to be somewhere Edward was afraid to go," she said. "Wait! He was afraid of the basement, remember? Let's look there next."

The girls searched the basement for half an hour. Finally George said, "We've covered every inch of the basement. I don't think the treasure is here."

"There's one more place Edward wouldn't go," Nancy said. "The attic."

The girls bounded up the stairs. Nancy tripped on the top stair and almost fell.

"Ow!" she cried, sitting down. "I stubbed my toe on that stupid nail again!"

She rubbed the tip of her shoe. "That nail is poking up. Maybe I should pull it out this time instead of putting it back in."

Nancy grabbed the nail and pulled hard. To her amazement, the top of the stair lifted up like a lid.

"It's a secret compartment," Bess whispered.

"It really *is* a secret," Nancy said. "I didn't even know it was here."

George opened the lid all the way. "There's something inside here!" she said.

Nancy lifted out a tin box with a flower pattern on it. "Someone hid this on purpose," she said excitedly. "I'll bet it's Amelia's treasure."

Gently she lifted the lid. But the box was empty.

"Edward really was a brat, I think," Nancy said. "He found Amelia's treasure after all!"

There was a lump in her throat. "I really wanted to find all the treasures," she said sadly.

"Now *you* don't have a treasure," Bess said. "That's not fair."

"We'll share our treasures with you," George said.

"That's okay," Nancy said. "I have the diary."

The three girls clomped down the stairs sadly. "Let's see what Hannah got us for lunch," Nancy said.

When Hannah saw the box, she said, "Where on earth did you find my old button box?"

"It's yours?" Nancy said.

Hannah turned the box over in her hands. "Yes. It disappeared when they were putting new floorboards in the attic. Where did you find it?"

"In a secret compartment at the top of the stairs," George explained.

"The carpenters put a new step on the top stair, too," Hannah said. "I used to have some sewing things in the attic. My button box must have gotten in that stair by accident."

"It's yours!" Nancy shouted, giving Hannah a big hug. "Hooray!"

"And why does that make you so happy?" Hannah asked with a smile.

"Because that means the box isn't Amelia's!" Nancy said. Suddenly she became serious. "Are there any bricks in the attic?" she asked Hannah.

"There's a brick chimney up there," Hannah said. "Look behind the old clothes chest by—"

But before she could finish, the girls had run back up the stairs.

Nancy wriggled behind the chest of drawers up in the attic. "Here's the chimney," she said.

She began feeling the bricks. "There's a loose one," she cried. She stuck her hand inside. "I have it! I'm sure it's the treasure!"

Acrylic Latex
Wall Flat Finish

"Well, hurry and come out so we can see it," Bess said.

Finally Nancy crawled out from behind the chest and stood up. She held out a small cameo brooch. "Amelia's grandmother gave this to her, remember?" she said.

"It's beautiful," Bess said.

"Here. Put it on," George said. She pinned the brooch to Nancy's blouse.

"I want to look at it in the mirror," Nancy said. She stood on her tiptoes so that she could see herself in the mirror above the chest. Then the girls went downstairs for lunch.

Hannah had fixed some tuna salad sandwiches for lunch. While they ate, the girls showed Mr. Drew the treasures.

"Now that we've found all the treasures, I'm ready to do my report on Amelia," Nancy said.

"Who are you two reporting on?" Mr. Drew asked Bess and George.

"My report is on Abraham Lincoln," Bess said. "He didn't move to Illinois until he was twenty-one years old. But he lived here until he was elected president."

"I picked Carl Sandburg," George told Mr. Drew. "He was a famous poet who lived in Chicago. Plus our school was named after him."

"I wish I knew what happened to Amelia when she grew up," Nancy said. "So far, I can only talk about her childhood."

Just then they heard the doorbell ring. "Can you get that, Nancy?" Mr. Drew said. He had a smile on his face.

"Sure, Daddy," Nancy said. She ran to the front door. When she opened the door, a woman and a man were standing there. Nancy didn't recognize them.

"Hello," the woman said. She was tall and thin, with light brown hair. She was wearing a red suit with navy blue shoes and a purse to match. "I'm looking for Nancy Drew," she said.

"That's me," Nancy replied.

"My name is Mrs. Fremont," the woman said. "I understand you have something of mine."

"I do?" Nancy said.

"Let me explain," Mrs. Fremont said. "Before my name was Fremont, it was Barton. I'm Amelia Barton. And I believe you have my diary."

Nancy was so shocked, she didn't know what to say.

"And there's my brooch!" Mrs. Fremont said, looking at Nancy's blouse.

# 8

# Found—and Lost Again

**Y**es, it's your brooch," Nancy blurted out. "We found your diary and all the hidden treasures, too. And we're sorry!"

To Nancy's surprise, Amelia Fremont smiled a big smile. "Good!" she exclaimed. "I'm happy you found everything."

Before Nancy could say anything, Mrs. Fremont turned to the man beside her. He was dressed in a gray suit and was wearing a hat.

"This is my brother, Edward," Mrs.

Fremont said. "You read about him, didn't you?"

Edward Barton took off his hat and bowed. "How do you do, young lady?" he said.

Nancy liked the twinkle in his eye. "How do you do?" she replied.

It's Edward the brat, she thought. But he's so polite. He doesn't seem like a brat.

"Your father invited us over," Amelia Fremont went on. "May we come in?"

"Oh! Oh, of course," Nancy said. She opened the door wide.

"Daddy!" she called out. "We have company."

Nancy turned around. There stood Mr. Drew with a big grin on his face. George and Bess were peeking out from behind him, their eyes wide.

Mr. Drew put his arm around Nancy's shoulder. "I didn't tell you I reached Mr. Barton, Nancy. He gave me Mrs. Fremont's number. I hope you don't mind. I wanted to surprise you."

"You did, Daddy." Nancy gulped. "But it's a wonderful surprise."

"Let's go sit down and talk," Mr. Drew said, leading everyone to the living room.

Nancy introduced Bess and George to Amelia Fremont and Edward Barton. "We're best friends," she explained to Mrs. Fremont. "Like you and Elizabeth and Ruth."

Mrs. Fremont's eyes glistened for a moment. Nancy thought she might start to cry.

"Elizabeth and Ruth and I are still friends, even though they moved away," Amelia Fremont told the girls. "We were your age when we hid our treasures."

She settled back in her chair. "Now," she said. "Tell me how you found them. Don't leave anything out."

Nancy and Bess and George took turns telling the whole story. Soon everyone was talking and laughing. Edward Barton loved the story about Aunt Tillie the best.

"We thought Aunt Tillie was a real aunt," Nancy said with a laugh.

Suddenly she stopped laughing.

"Are you mad that I told my teacher about your diary?" she asked Amelia Fremont.

"Oh, no," Mrs. Fremont said, shaking her head. "Believe me, I don't mind if anyone reads it now."

She paused and looked at the three friends. "And that's not all," she said. "I told Elizabeth and Ruth that you found our treasures, and we all agree. We want you girls to keep them."

"You mean it?" Bess exclaimed. "Oh, thank you!"

George looked down at her ring and smiled.

Nancy gulped. She had something to say that might make everyone mad at her.

"Thank you, Mrs. Fremont," Nancy said. "I hope you don't mind, but I've been thinking about something." She squirmed in her chair. "I . . . I'd like to put everything back."

"You would?" George asked.

"But why?" Bess asked, clutching the charm on Elizabeth's necklace.

"Well, this way other people might

find the diary," Nancy began. "And if they do, maybe they'll follow the clues in it and find the hidden treasures again."

Nancy looked at Bess and George. "They would have as much fun as we did finding the treasures."

Everyone in the room sat quietly for a moment.

Finally George said, "That's a great idea, Nancy."

"I guess I think so, too," Bess said. Then she brightened up. "But I still hate to give up Aunt Tillie." Everyone laughed.

Amelia Fremont nodded her head. "It's a splendid idea, Nancy. But before you put the diary back, could you do something for me."

Nancy nodded.

"I'd like it if you three girls wrote in it—something about your friendship."

"I like that idea," Nancy said. "If someone else finds the diary, maybe she will write about her friends, too."

Edward Barton had been looking

through the diary. "How could you write such awful things about me, Sis?" he said. "You called me a brat!"

He pretended to be hurt. Then his eyes twinkled. "And I was!" he told the girls.

After Amelia Fremont and Edward Barton left, Nancy hugged her father. "Thanks, Daddy. It was great to meet Amelia."

"Now you can do your report on her whole life," Mr. Drew said.

"Oh, right! My report," Nancy said. She turned to Bess and George. "We'd better finish them."

"And write in Amelia's diary," Bess reminded her.

When Bess and George left that afternoon, Nancy gave them each a big hug. "I know we will always be friends like Amelia and Elizabeth and Ruth," she told them. "But I still hope you never move!"

On Monday morning Nancy couldn't wait for social studies. That's when

Mrs. Reynolds's students were giving their oral reports.

"Well, class, who wants to give the first report?" Mrs. Reynolds asked. Nancy raised her hand high.

"All right, Nancy," Mrs. Reynolds said. "Go ahead."

Nancy walked to the head of the class. "My report is on Amelia Barton," she began. "She's not a famous person. But she lived in my house fifty years ago. Now she lives near Chicago."

Nancy held up the diary. "I met Amelia through this book," she went on. "It's a diary that she kept in 1943. She was my age then—-eight years old."

Nancy described finding the diary and the treasures. Then she held up a photo of Amelia and her family. "This is Amelia now. I met her and Edward yesterday. My dad and I found her, using our computer."

Nancy told the class about Amelia's children and grandchildren and everything she could remember from the diary and Amelia herself.

When Nancy finished, the class clapped. Everyone, that is, except Brenda Carlton.

"Excellent, Nancy," Mrs. Reynolds said. "You certainly found someone different to report on."

Brenda glared at Nancy as she headed back to her seat. "I knew this was a good story," Brenda whispered to her. "It's all your fault I didn't get to write it up for my newspaper."

Nancy smiled. "You should look for loose bricks," she whispered. She giggled and slid into her seat. "Good stories are always hiding behind them."

That evening, Nancy put the diary back behind the brick. The next day the workers were going to put more plaster on the wall.

Then, just before she went to sleep, Nancy opened her blue notebook. She found the page for "The Hidden Treasures Mystery." At the bottom she wrote:

I learned something this weekend. Sometimes the best thing about finding a treasure is not keeping it. Sometimes it's more fun to leave it for others to find, too.

Case closed. (Unless someone else opens it in fifty years!)

**Do your younger brothers and sisters
want to read books like yours?**

**Let them know there
are books just for _them_!**

They can join Nancy Drew and her best
friends as they collect clues and solve
mysteries in

# THE

# NANCY DREW

# NOTEBOOKS®

Starting with

#1 The Slumber Party Secret

#2 The Lost Locket

#3 The Secret Santa

#4 Bad Day for Ballet

**AND**

**Meet up with suspense and mystery
in The Hardy Boys® are: The Clues Brothers™**

Starting with

#1 The Gross Ghost Mystery

#2 The Karate Clue

#3 First Day, Worst Day

#4 Jump Shot Detectives

A MINSTREL® BOOK

Published by Pocket Books

*Split-second suspense...*
*Brain-teasing puzzles...*

# No case is too tough for the world's greatest teen detective!

# NANCY DREW®

## MYSTERY STORIES

## By Carolyn Keene

*Join Nancy and her friends in*
*thrilling stories of adventure and intrigue*

Look for brand-new mysteries
wherever books are sold

Available from Minstrel® Books
Published by Pocket Books

# BILL WALLACE

Award-winning author Bill Wallace brings you fun-filled
animal stories full of humor and exciting adventures.

A MINSTREL® BOOK

Published by Pocket Books